KATIE THE CATSITTER

Random House New York

Katie the Catsitter

Colleen
AF Venable

ILLUSTRATED BY
Stephanie Yue

WITH COLORS BY
Braden Lamb

This is a work of fiction. Names, characters, places, and incidents either are the product of the author's imagination or are used fictitiously. Any resemblance to actual persons, living or dead, events, or locales is entirely coincidental.

Special thanks to coloring assistants, Shelli Paroline and Sam Bennett

Visit us on the Web! rhcbooks.com

Educators and librarians, for a variety of teaching tools, visit us at RHTeachersLibrarians.com

Library of Congress Cataloging-in-Publication Data is available upon request.
ISBN 978-0-593-30632-1 (hardcover)
ISBN 978-1-9848-9563-9 (pbk.)
ISBN 978-1-9848-9564-6 (lib. bdg.)
ISBN 978-1-9848-9565-3 (ebook)

Book design by Stephanie Yue and Sylvia Bi

MANUFACTURED IN CHINA
10 9 8 7 6 5 4 3 2 1
First Edition

To Teri, Mrs. B, and all the other brave souls who gave me pet-sitting, babysitting, and other odd jobs as a kid.
P.S. I'm sorry I killed all your plants.

—C.A.F.V.

To Hotpot, Cho Cho, Cleopatra, Mayhem, and Ginger, mayor of Central Square. To all the cats still with us, all the cats who have left us, and all the cats I have yet to meet.

—S.Y.

CHAPTER ONE

CHK!
Oof.
POP
Ow.

Oh, hello, keys. I see you decided to stay home today.

Sorry, Katie-Cat! Didn't get a
chance to get groceries, but
promise I'll bring you some
poppers from work for
breakfast. If you're hu
treat yourself to some o
the Fun Fund. Love you!
XO –Mom

DOWNSTAIRS AT MR. B'S BODEGA
OPEN
BING BONG

THUMP

Fun Fund?

Woo, fun. Are coins even *considered* money anymore?

I'm with you, Scratch-Off.

How 'bout baby kale . . .
blue cheese . . . Craisins . . .
those are basically candy!
Caaandy.

Fiiiine.
HISS!

You know *vegetarian* has the word *veggie* in it?
It's not my fault your PB&Js are magical, Mr. B.

I'm here at the New You Cosmetics factory, where a fire is raging. Sources described a loud, explosive noise.
Police Chief Pardo is here with more. Chief, what do you think happened?

Criminals! Supervillains! Hear me now! You messed with the wrong police force—

EEK!
THE EASTERN SCREECH!

Yes. It is I.
What a pleasure! As New York's highest Yelp-rated superhero, what's your take on the fire?

This. Is no accident. This fire. Burns like indigestion from a justice burrito.

Obviously, someone thought this building . . . was ugly.

The windows. Were all wrong. And the brick color clashed with . . .
Um . . . Eastern Screech . . .

I don't think it was the brick color.

Seriously, like hundreds of rabbits!
Must have been some sort of animal testing. I wonder what's going to happen to them.

Pretty sure Chief Pardo kept them all. You should have seen his face. I didn't even know that guy had smile muscles!
And Owl Guy. He's so dumb. I can't believe Jess thinks he's hot!

Didn't she pay attention during science when we learned about owl pellets?
"Hey, Jessica, I got you a gift *hurk!* Spoiler. My vomit is a mouse."
Haha! I'm going to miss you.

You know I'm going to write every day.
I know. It's just that I get so bored when you're away.

Nothing ever happens around here.

LABYRINTH

You're still awake?

Thought you might want a hot breakfast to kick off your last week of school.

Marcus made it special at the end of my shift, so when I say hot, I mean HOT.
Too hot.

Too hot? No such thing!

I'm in heaven.

I will never understand your iron stomach.
Eff you can 'eel ya 'ongue, it's 'ot 'ot enough.

Anything exciting happen last night?
GLUG GLUG

Did you see the news? About that factory? There were like A HUNDRED rabbits that got out, and Chief Pardo turned into a mushy pile of muscly goo! And . . .

zZZ

z z Z

CHAPTER TWO

There's so much we can learn from the Eastern Screech. Last night he put himself at risk to save hundreds of poor rabbits from a terrible fire. I'd like to use today's art session to honor him and all animals in general. His ability to get in touch with nature and the majestic owl is one of the things that makes him noble, intelligent, quick, mysterious, handsome . . .

. . . likely single, I mean I've never noticed a ring on his wings. . . .

Other than the subway system. Did I tell you I was stuck for twenty minutes at West Fourth the other day?! Twenty minutes! And there were these annoying dancers and someone was eating a bag of chips with their mouth open and this one guy was practically doing a SPLIT to take up two seats. . . .

How is it possible for Ms. Sistine to be both a hippie and high-strung at the same time?
123!

Jess!
What's 123?

The number of hours left till camp! Go, Camp Bear Lake! *Grrrrrowl.*
Oh.
Do you think Theo is going to be there again? His acne was kinda legendary, but I'm pretty sure there's a total hottie under there.

Be one with nature! Embrace the void! Smell the manure!
What are you gonna draw?
A cow? Something has to make the manure we're supposed to smell.

I'm gonna draw that red-tailed hawk we saw last summer. Remember when we were hiking Mount . . .

Jess! Enough about camp!
No, it's okay. I'd be excited too . . . if I was going.

You should totally come! Bethany, don't you think she should come? There's four weeks. I bet you can get into one of them. I'm sure they can find some space for you!
Yeah, it's not really a space issue.

Jess has a point. You don't have to go to ALL the sessions. It would be so much fun to have you there for one! Maybe the week of the canoe races? Or nocturnal week, where we get to stay up crazy late!
It'd be so fun! I can get my mom to spot you for one week. . . .

I should really focus on my cow.

Don't be afraid to let inspiration swim through the coral tunnels of your brain.

Uh. Okay.

Maybe you could get a summer job and save up the money?
Pretty sure no one's gonna hire a twelve-year-old.

Actually . . .
. . . maybe they would . . .

See, now THIS is art.

Does it really bother you if I talk about camp, Katie? Because if it does, I'll totally stop.
Naw. It's okay. I think I have a plan.

In that case, 122 hours!

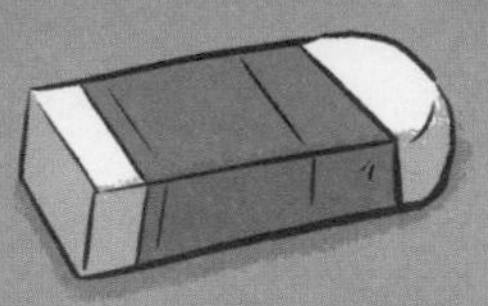

Help Katie go to camp!

Hey, I'm Katie! I've lived in the city my entire life. With YOUR help I can see my first real forest! Breathe fresh air! See animals that aren't pigeons or rats! Learn how to hike, canoe, and capture a flag (not sure what that means but I've been told it's fun).

I live in your building, and I'm ready to help with anything you need!

Water your plants!

Clean your apartment!

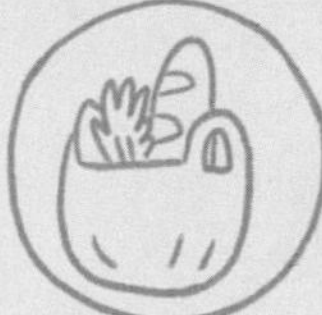

Carry groceries!

Anything! No job too big or too small!

AFTER SCHOOL

Help Katie go to camp!

Help Katie go to camp!
I live in your building and
I'm ready to help with anything you need!

Carrying groceries. Hmm. I'll hire ya! Went to camp myself as a kid!

How does $2 a bag sound?
GREAT!

Sixth floor, 6F. I'll race ya!
Ooof.
THUD

I WIN!

There ya are. Was getting worried.
2nd Floor

Shoulda warned ya it was protein shake day! Here's a dollar for making it halfway. Why don't ya go and grab the light one!
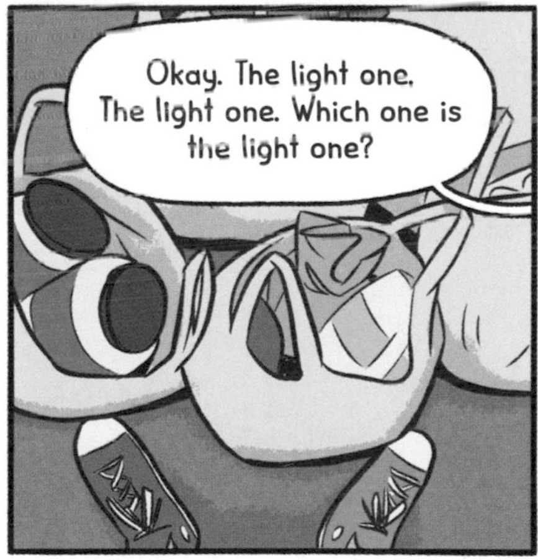
Okay. The light one. The light one. Which one is the light one?

Nope.

CRACK

Sigh. Found it.

Sorry

SKCH
SKCH
SKCH

Help Katie go to camp!
Hey, I'm Katie! I've lived in the city my entire life.
With YOUR help I can see my first real forest! Breathe
fresh air! See animals that aren't pigeons or rats!
Learn how to hike, canoe, and capture a flag (not sure
what that means but I've been told it's fun).

I live in your building, and
I'm ready to help with anything you need!
Water your plants!

Clean your apartment!

Anything! No job too big or too small!

LABYRINTH

KNOCK-KNOCK!

Hello?

Oh, good! You're home.
KITTY!
It's KATIE. Kay-tee.
KITTY!!

Hi, Mrs. Bell. Hi, Marcie. Hi, Dink-Dink.
Don't encourage her.
DINK-DINK!
Sorry. Hi, Dimitri.

I'm leaving for my in-laws' in fifteen and my brain is all over the place. Saw your sign. Would you be willing to water my houseplants till the weekend?
YES! That would be amazing!

Fantastic. Let's say $10 a day. Here's the spare key. No need to water the succulents. The fern needs some love, and the terrarium just needs two spray bottle spritzes, but fast ones like "spritz spritz." The moss ball needs to be soaked for five minutes, but just the moss part. DON'T wet the top leaves or it gets moldy. Got it?
Yes?

Actually, can you repeat . . .
Phew! You're a lifesaver, Katie.
Bye, KITTY!

Oh, and I almost forgot. Mr. Quinn from 6F asked me to give you this.

See you Friday!

Sorry
YOU EARNED THIS PLEASE KEEP IT
P.S. DON'T WRITE ON CURRENCY

CAMP
FUN FUND

TUESDAY
QUADRATIC FORMULA
Pizza Pi
I'd retire, but I don't want to experience the AFTERMATH.
98!

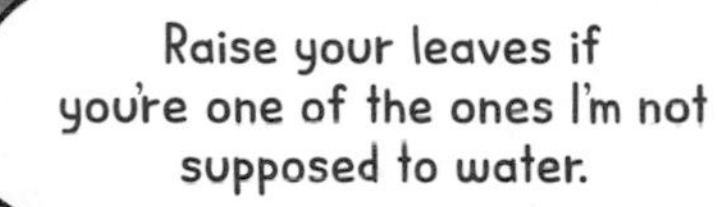
Raise your leaves if you're one of the ones I'm not supposed to water.

WEDNESDAY
71!
Groowl!

Ready for your five minute soak, Mr. Moss Ball? At least this one is easy.

THURSDAY

FRIDAY

Help Katie go to camp!

Hey, I'm Katie! I've lived in the city my entire life. With YOUR help I can see my first real forest! Breathe fresh air! See animals that aren't pigeons or rats! Learn how to hike, canoe, and capture a flag (not sure what that means but I've been told it's fun).

I live in your building, and I'm ready to help with anything you need!

3 P.M. LAST DAY OF SCHOOL

EACHERS' LOUNGE

Schoooool's out
fa summma.

Maybe I can convince Counselor Mark to teach me how to play guitar.
How's the Camp Fun Fund going?

We could start a band . . . maybe go on tour . . .
It's . . . going.

NERD!
Whatever, fart breath!

You know, I think I want to take the subway today.

I'll miss you! AND we'll see you for the last session, right? Get ready for more s'mores than one person should ever eat!

18!

I'm so jealous of you. There's so many free things in NY in the summer! Movies in the park. Shakespeare in the Park. Renting bikes . . .
In the park?

I wanna see REAL nature. Not just nature planted by old rich dudes.
SHOWTIME! SHOWTIME!
Ugh.

How's the saving REALLY going?
Made a whole dollar.

Hahaha!
AIR HORN

THWUMPA

Oh. Well, a dollar is a start!

How're your break-dancing skills? Those showtime dancers just made like twenty bucks.
Minus the cost of the lost shoe.

I think most of that was bribery money to make them stop.
I SCREECH for it!

Afternoon, Ms. Beth.
Bethany.

There's only ten kids in the building! You'd think he could get my name right.
You're lucky. The oldest kid in my building is a fourth of my age.

Don't.
But how will we know what it does if we don't push it?!

5
6
3
4
1
2
DO NOT PRESS

I still say it turns the elevator into a rocket like in *Charlie and the Chocolate Factory*.
And I say it turns me into a grounded kid.
Perfect timing!

Happy summer vacation!
YESSSS.

Geez, Katie!

I gotta eat two months' worth of cookies before you guys leave.
Oh. What is this piece of paper I have just discovered in my hand?

I have found a voucher. It says it pays for a single session at camp. So random!

Wow. You are the worst actor, Mom.
Come on, Katie! Just let me pay for one week. You'll love it!

It's okay, Mrs. Tinoco. I want to raise the money myself.
I HAD to try. We play games all day long, learn these cool crafts, swim in this giant lake . . . but it's never as fun as it could be because you aren't there!

Well, then I guess I have to be there this summer.

I wish you would let me help. But at least I have another surprise for you.

Just got off the phone with your mom.

Wish granted.
DAZZLING HAIR
BRIGHT COLOR
TEAL
YES!!!!
WHOA!

TEAL

Eight suitcases? It's just one night!
I don't want to run out of jigsaw puzzles.

Hey! I got you something.

Now we have a matching set. You better up your postcard game this year!
There's no way I could dethrone the Sticker Queen.

All must bow down before my puffy glitter kitten power!
Hmm. Mousetress burned down another factory.

Again? When are they going to catch that vile woman?! Katie. Promise me you'll be safe this summer.
Don't go out late at night. This world is overflowing with unqualified people in ill-fitting spandex, and I think it's cutting off all the circulation to their brain cells.

I'll write every day.

Twice a day?

Deal!

Help Katie g

o camp!
my entire life.
forest! Breathe
geons or rats!
a flag (not sure
fun).

Help Katie go to camp!
I can do this.

CHAPTER THREE

3A
3A
4F
4F
5D
5D
6B
SNFF
SNFF
6B

Help Katie go to camp!
Hey, I'm Katie! I've lived in the city my entire life. With YOUR help I can see my first real forest! Breathe fresh air! See animals that aren't pigeons or rats! Learn how to hike, canoe, and capture a flag (not sure what that means but I've been told it's fun).
Anything! No job too big or too small!

Nature is overrated.
Help Katie go to camp!

It's just not fair.

Life isn't fair. For instance, the health department unfairly doesn't love when people put their face germs on my counter.

I mean, how fun could camp really be?

There are mosquitoes! Ticks! Other bugs I don't even know the names of because I only ever see cockroaches! Gah! I don't even get to see new bugs!
AHH!
HISS!

I used to go to camp for the whole summer when I was a kid. The air just tasted better upstate. Camping on top of that mountain made me feel like the world was this magical place.
Met some of the best friends of my life there.

And this makes me feel better how? I wish I could have a cat. THAT would make me feel better.

It wasn't all good. I basically spent two months every year covered in poison ivy.

Scratch-Off! Leave that nice man alone!

TAK

Watch out!

???

PURRPRRPURRPU
URRP
RPR
PURR
UR
RP
TUR
RR
PR
RR
UP
PUR

Hello, Vincent.
Five p.m.? Isn't it a bit early for you, Madeline?
PRR
PRR

I wouldn't do that, dear. He's not the friendliest of ca–

Interesting.

Okay, that joke only works when you say "hey." But you get my point. Enjoy the summer!

CHAPTER FOUR

I said no pets!
Huh?

You sound like you live with elephants! Walk quieter!

Sorry, Mrs. Piper.

Elephants!!!

5B

Ah. There you are. I'm so glad.
AH!

Tonight I'll be working till midnight. I'm actually running a bit late already.
How does $25 an hour sound?
Um . . .
Okay, okay. $30?

For . . . what?
Goodness! Got ahead of myself.

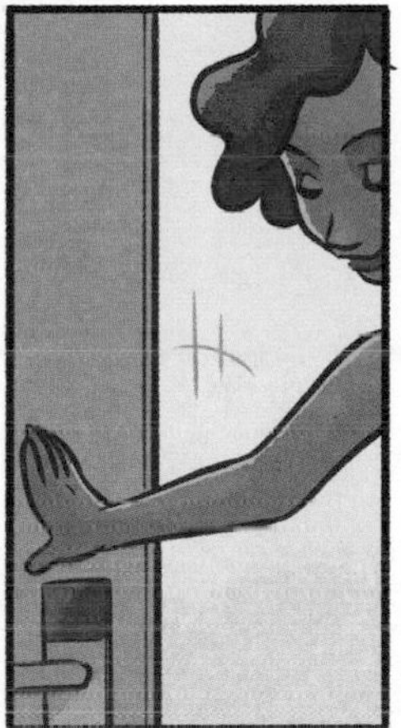

I need a cat sitter.

Mrs. Piper let you have . . .
GASP
. . . two cats?!

Wrong and wrong. Mrs. Piper doesn't know.
And . . .

. . . it's more than two cats.

Please come in. Miles! Gracie! Admiral Dewey! Get our guest some refreshments.

How many are there?
Just 217.

217!
Sadly, New York City apartments just don't fit 218 cats well.

You trained them to fetch?
Teaching a cat to fetch is easy.

Jolie, we need another house key.
CLAP CLAP

Jolie, no hacking the Pentagon tonight.
Mewrew.
SCAN

IS THAT CAT USING A COMPUTER?!
Teaching a cat to hit a few keys is easy.

Smooch will show you how to use the remote.

Just no scary movies. Oslo gets nightmares.
Meorow!

Is cash okay?
Uh . . . sure . . . but what do I have to do? Feed them? Clean the litter box . . . es?

How many litter boxes ARE there?!

Ha! Litter boxes. No, they don't use those.

Meow.
Meow.

Oh, good. It's done.

Everything in my apartment locks and unlocks by fingerprint scanner, so here's your key.

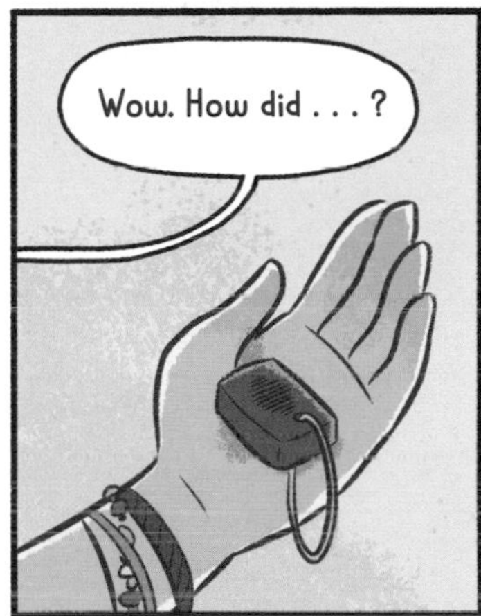
Wow. How did . . . ?

Teaching a cat to create a 3-D model, render and print a mold, then cast and cure a silicone fingerprint is easy.

I'm off! There's a list on the fridge with emergency contact information and all their names. I'll be home at midnight.

Be good, kitties.
Wait . . . I . . .

CLICK!

PURR
PURR
PURR
PURR

This is . . .

. . . amazing.

SCRATCH SCRATC

SCRATCH SCRATC

CRATCH SCRATCH

No, no, no. Ms. Lang is going to kill me!

HA! Too quick for you!
BZZZT!
CRASH!
SHATTER

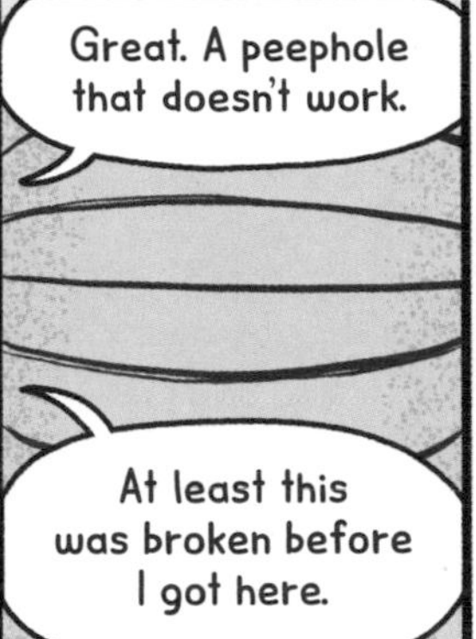

Great. A peephole that doesn't work.
At least this was broken before I got here.

Pizza delivery.

I didn't order any . . .

e-buy
Jet Engine Like New!
BUY!

HEY! NO BUYING
JET ENGINES!

DING DING
BZZZZZZT!
CLICK

KNOCK
KNOCK
Mom
Hey, Katie-Cat! How's Operation Camp Fund going? Any jobs?

I told you I didn't order these pizzas.

WHAT IS GOING ON HERE?

They aren't my cats!
CATS?!

Cats! What cats?

Cats? I didn't say cats.
I said . . . gnats?
Aaah!
Uh, rats?
AAAAAHH!
No, THAT'S. That's a nice robe. That's what I said.

It was Mr. Piper's.
I hate flowers.
What are you doing here? You don't live here!
I'm, uh . . .

. . . cleaning?

Clean QUIETER.

SLAM

BOING!

Ack!

Why did I think
I could do this?

CLICK!

Why did I think I could do
ANYTHING?

BLECH!

I'm never watching a cute cat video again! You hear that, cats? You ruined the internet!

Nine minutes till I get fired. Again. I bet Bethany and Jess are melting s'mores right now and forgetting all about me.

Guys?

GUYS?!
Oh no, no, no, no.

How do you lose 217 cats?!

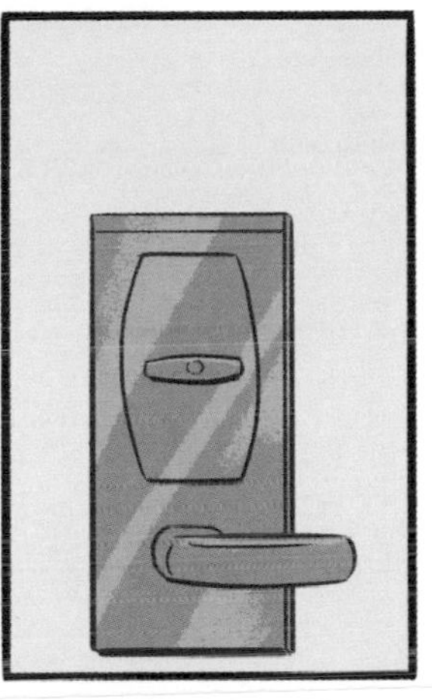

Are those . . .
couch pillows?

Where did you . . . ?

TWO MINUTES EARLIER
Weird kid.

I thought I had
a couch here.

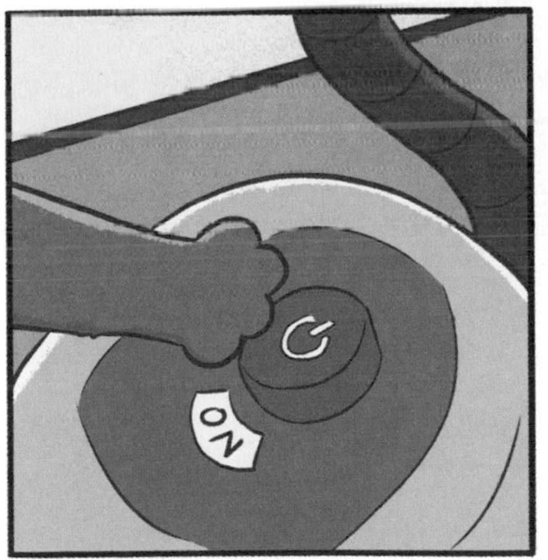
ON

VRRRRRMM

Interesting.
AH!

I'm so sorry! I didn't know what to do! There are just so many of them and . . .
I've never seen the apartment so clean!

As promised.

Same time tomorrow night?

3B

CAMP
BEARLAKE

CAMP
FUN FUND

Hi, Katie-Cat!
Pretty boring here in the woods.
Chipmunks keep asking about you.
Chitter chitter chitter. That's Max.
He says he really wants to meet
you and also if you come you
should bring some acorns. Like
LOTS of acorns. How's the odd-
job business going? Miss you
like TONS! Jess is already driving
me batty. Pretty sure there's
not a single boy here that she
doesn't have a crush on.
Max included.
MISS YOU!!!!
Bethany Isabella
Katie Spera
5965 Ave D, Apt 3B
New York, NY 10009

Hmm. Well, that's a new style.
I will never get fashion.

Please, don't be a
teenager. Not yet.

CHAPTER FIVE

TRY IT NOW, COUCH THIEF! MUAHAHA! MUAHA . . .
HUH?
I'm home!
Hello, kitties!

I'm not exaggerating! There are 217 cats in her apartment!
I believe you that there are a lot . . . she's definitely an eccentric. But 217? You actually counted?

Of coooourse I have. They totally stand still for me.

There's this orange one that keeps buying things online, and a gray-and-white one that keeps changing the channel to scary movies, and a black-and-brown one that seems to HATE glassware.

What are their names?
I don't know. Evil, Evil, and So-Evil-That-Evil-Is-Not-a-Strong-Enough-Word Evil?

Maybe if you take the time to learn their names, they might be more responsive.

You're the worst when you're right.

THAT EVENING . . .
All right, let's see. . . .

Jolie. White with black and brown spots.
Fashion designer
Jolie
White with black and brown
spots. Likes: hacking
modeling, online
Gracie
Likes: hacking, 3-D modeling, online gaming.

Jolie: Computer Hacking
TAP TAP TAP
Why are you raiding our village?! We're on the same team!

Okaaaay.

Hmm . . . I think you're Gracie? Says here you can understand and interpret eighty-two languages.

Hola, Gracie.
Uh . . . ¿Dónde
está el baño?

Gracie: Language Expert
MIAU

Lyapa
Master of various martial arts and weapons
Mackerel
Semaphore expert

Lyapa: Master of various martial arts and weapons?

Lyapa: Weapons Expert

Jujitsu? Lock-picking? Helicopter repair? Counterattacks?

Camouflage? Smoke bombs? Bath bombs? Getaway driver?! What is this list?!

At least THIS one is normal. Miles: Long black cat, bright green eyes, loves lasers.
Yoga instructor
Miles
Long black cat, bright green eyes, loves lasers.
Minnie

Which one of you is Miles?

There you are! Do you want to play? Let's play!

CLICK

CLICK

death of me! Or the lake mon-
ster. Personally, I prefer the lake
monster. MISS YOU!!! SAVE ME FROM
THIS BASKET!
—Bethany!
5965 Ave D, Apt 3B
New York, NY 10009
Katie,
Don't worry if you don't raise the
money! I miss you every day and
we can always go to camp next
year. To make you feel better here
are the places I currently have
mosquito bites: arms, legs, back
of knee, hand, stomach, foot, my
ear . . . Yes, that's right, you can
get mosquito bites on YOUR EAR!
I'm pretty sure I heard Max the
chipmunk laughing at me when
that one happened. I jumped
10 feet out of my sleeping
bag. MISS YOOOUU!!! Bethany!
Katie Spera
5965 Ave D, Apt 3B
New York, NY 10009
Bethany,
If you ever wonder how much I value
your friendship, please measure it in
cats. 217 cats. That's how much I care
about you. Can't wait to tell you more
about this job, but GOOD NEWS!!!! At
this rate I should have the money by
nocturnal week!!! Ya know, if I don't
get murdered by lasers or evil ... first.
HEARTS!

CHAPTER SIX

I'm telling you! The cats are evil.
All cats are a little evil. That's what makes them cats.

But these are like SUPERVILLAIN-level! GASP! Maybe they are supervillains! I should warn Ms. Lang!

Have you checked the database?
Good idea!

Come on! Load! When are we going to upgrade this thing?!
We're locked into a really great rate!
Yeah, two hundred years ago. Our router is older than Mrs. Piper!

That reminds me. Have you seen anyone walking out of the building carrying a couch?
Mrs. Piper is CONVINCED there's a couch thief on the loose. Haha.

Huh. Yeah. Weird.

NYC SUPERHERO VILLAIN

NYC SUPERHERO VILLAIN

evil cats
S

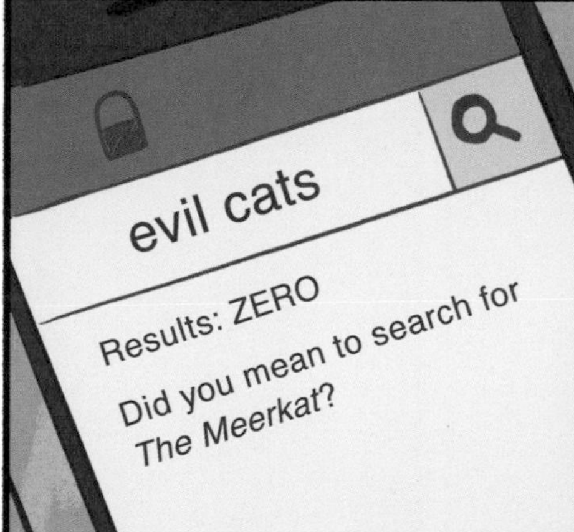
evil cats
Results: ZERO
Did you mean to search for
The Meerkat?

Katie!

Yo-yos are really boring to play with. They had a yo-yo expert come to camp to teach us tricks, but the only thing I learned was how uncool you look doing yo-yo tricks in the woods. Max says chitter chitter, which means he wants you to up his acorn allotment because he's been weight lifting. Saw him lift a shoe twice his size! It was Jess's shoe. Now she won't wear it. Trying my best to not laugh at her hopping around on one foot. Wonder if Counselor Mark finds hopping attractive. I WANT TO HEAR ALL ABOUT THIS NEW JOB!!! I'm so excited you are saving up the money!!!

GET HERE ALREADY!
Bethany

Katie Spera
5965 Ave D, Apt 3B
New York, NY 10009

Nox: Robotics Expert

DJ Bootie Butler: Mad Beats

Pierogi: Textiles Expert
CLICK
CLICK
CLICK

Beedee: High Jump

5B

WARNING:
CONTENTS SUPER
COMBUSTIBLE
UP
I don't care what it is! Send it back! Send it back!
5B

MONDAY
Yesssss.

Two!

WEDNESDAY
Postcard.

Postcard.

SATURDAY
Postcard.

Giant wad of glitter.

Possibly attached to postcard but I'm too blind from glitter to tell.

But I need the money! The more I work, the faster I get to camp!

How about tonight I help out. I've got the night off. It's been a while since I changed a litter box, but I think it'll come back to me.

You do NOT want to meet these cats. Also, they don't use litter boxes.

They aren't litter-box trained? No wonder you're so stressed!

Got my Benadryl, some treats, and I bought a few cat toys. I'm ready!
5B

Trust me. You are NOT ready.

Awwww. Look at all these cuties!

I know it's a lot of them, but they couldn't be sweeter!
Maybe you've just been hanging out with Scratch-Off too much and forgot what a nice cat is like!

I still can't get over that they use the bathroom. Cats using the bathroom!

And I can't get over how nice they're being. It's almost like it's a trick.

Hello, my fur babies! I'm home! Oh, hi, Cheryl. Lovely to see you!

Thought Katie could use some help, but these are the most well-behaved cats I've ever seen!
I've trained them well.

Here you go! And some chocolates I got at work tonight.
So thoughtful!

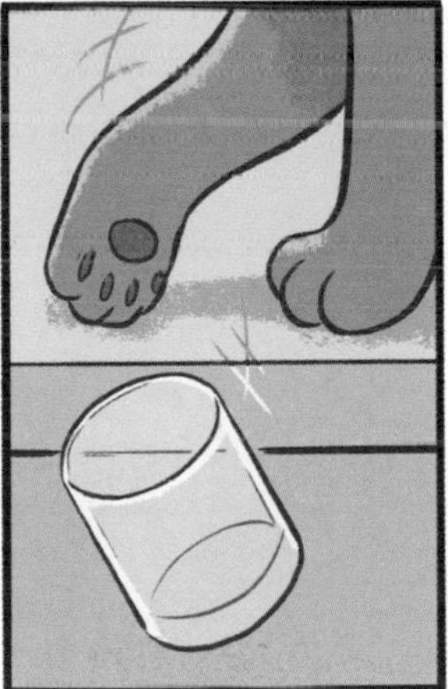

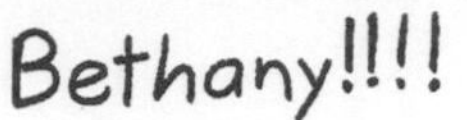

Bethany!!!!

Okay, so good news is I'm only six nights of cat sitting away from my camp money goal! I can't wait to see you (and Max, of course—please tell him chitter chitter chitter, he'll understand).

I don't know how it's possible, but I swear the cats are EVEN MORE evil than usual. I feel like they're plotting something. Something big. I can't figure out how to outsmart them! They've stolen at least 9 couches from Mrs. Piper, and she's bound to figure it out eventually. What should I doooooo?

Not a couch thief,
just an accessory to
couch thief-ery,

Katie

Katie the Cat Conqueror—

You're smart! You're fast! You're tall . . . well, maybe not that last one. You can play some tricks on THEM before they get a chance to play a trick on you. Remember that fifteen-minute trick we used to do to the clock in Ms. Sistine's room?

Max says you should try bribery first. Also, he says there's a boy named Ben who's not the worst. He's got these crazy dark brown eyes that are like melty. I think I might have a crush. On Ben. Not Max. Because that would be weird.

Cannot WAIT for you to meet everyone. Conquer the kitties, then come join me!!! I've perfected my s'more game. The trick is heating up the graham cracker TOO so the chocolate melts on both sides. I'll make you a Bethany Original!

—Bethany

CHAPTER SEVEN

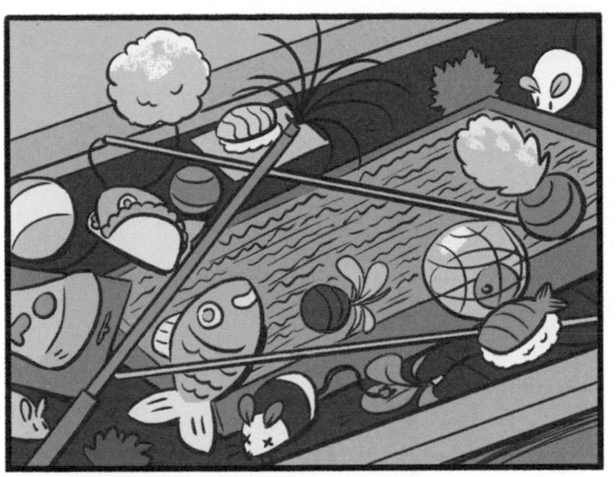

Aaaaahhhh!!!

Tell my mother
I love . . .

. . . when I get to say
"Told ya so."

Who wants to go fishing?!

PURE ORGANICS CHOCOLATE, just last week the industry leader in gourmet sweets, is now officially out of business thanks to a shocking discovery.

The explosion is still being investigated, but it isn't the only thing under investigation. A company that prides itself on ethical farming isn't so ethical after all!

Don't worry about this wall! I like it like this. It's fine . . . DON'T TOUCH IT!

. . . but instead was using the trips to illegally hunt animals. Endangered animals. Animals she THEN put on display in a secret office.

Who wants to play with laser pointers?

Out, darn spots!

Hi, Kitty!
Hey, Marcie.

I saw a giiiiiiant mouse!
Eww! Really? In your apartment?!

No, silly! She was ON the apartment. Then she flew off.

Pfhoooooo!

MARCIE! Who are you talking to?
It's Kitty! She's coming down. I'm telling her about the big mouse!

Hi, Katie.
I'M SO SORRY ABOUT THE PLANTS!!!
I've got two kids. It's amazing the plants lived as long as they did.

Besides, they're already coming back.

That's so great! If you need me to help again–
NO!

Uh, I mean, no, thanks. Marcie, get back inside.
I gotta go, Kitty!

Here! The mouse gave me chocolate!

I think it's time for Plan B.

CLK
CLK

CLICK
CLICK

Oh, look. It's 11:59.

CLICK

Haha!

CLICK

Well, look at that. Seems the clocks were wrong.
11:50

HA HA HA HA
HA HA HA

CHAPTER EIGHT

You should have seen your faces when the vacuum turned on.
Looks like no more stealing couches for you!

Here, I'll help.

I lost my parents when
I was very young.
CNEN Exclusive Interview with
New York City's Greatest Superhero

That was ONE TIME. At the
mall. FOR FIVE MINUTES.

I can't believe THAT GUY is
our best hero.
Did someone say something?
I can only hear . . . my heart.
Re-breaking.

I'm making popcorn.
Who's in?

We interrupt this interview for a special report.
BREAKING NEWS:
SPECIAL REPORT

Last night a robbery took place. The victim? Hunter Q. Prescott—musician, actor, philanthropist, and sorta slam poet.

Yeah, Girl-Bro. They took my TV, my rad audio setup, even my fave sunglahs right off my eyeballs.
The sunglasses are Hunter's custom-made Gocheez, a vital and EXPENSIVE part of his signature look.

I've got a poem for you, thief! Roses are red, violets are blue. Gimme my glasses back, because . . . something something goo?

A witness—who identified as "TOTALLY NOT A STALKER HIDING IN THE BUSH BY HUNTER'S WESTERN WINDOW"—claims they saw a mouse-shaped silhouette on the roof. Could this be the work of New York's most dangerous supervillain?!

The Mousetress is still at large, and VERY, VERY dangerous. Like super-duper dangero–

Phew, what a night!

CLICK!

Didn't mean to startle you. I really need to make more noise when I move. Haha.

HAHAHA.

HAHA, GOOD ONE.
5B

HA. BYE!
5B

While searching for clues, the police uncovered a secret trap door in the living room.

BREAKING NEWS:
Hunter "Questionable" Prescott?

And it *wasn't* a superhero lair.

Turns out Mr. Prescott's billions don't come from his albums or sweet dance moves.

OR MY POETRY!

Prescott was running an illegal gambling ring specializing in dogfighting. Chief Pardo is here with more.

Bethany!!! I haven't heard from you in
forever. Is everything okay? I'm finally
getting a handle on all the cats, though
that's the least of my troubles right now.
Brace yourself for this, but I'm starting
to think Ms. Lang is THE MOUSETRESS.
Seriously! She had Hunter Q. Prescott's
sunglasses in her place, and it explains why
she's out every night and never talks about
her job. That's because her job is CRIME!
CRIIIIIIIME!!! What am I gonna do? Should
I confront her? I wish you were here to
help me figure out what to do!!! I miss you.
Please write back as soon as possible!!!!

Hearts and Cats and Eeeeeeee,
Katie

Bethany Tinoco
Camp Bear Lake
Grosbeak Road
Bear Lake Valley, NY

PRESS

SHUNK
SHWOOP!

PHTOO

Interesting.
ethany!!! I haven't heard from you
forever. Is everything okay? I'm
finally getting a handle on all the
cats, though that's the least of my
troubles right now. Brace yourself for
this, but I'm starting to think Ms. Lang
is THE MOUSETRESS. Seriously! She
had Hunter Q. Prescott's sunglasses in
her place, and it explains why she's out
every night and never talks about her
job. That's because her job is CRIME!
CRIIIIIIIME!!! What am I gonna do?
Should I confront her? I wish you were
here to help me figure out what to
do!!! I miss you. Please write back
as soon as possible!!!!
Hearts and Cats and Eeeeeeee,
Katie
Bethany
Camp Bear Lake
Grosbeak Road
Bear Lake Valley, NY

CHAPTER NINE

Hey, has the mail dude been by yet today?

He has a name.
What's his name?

Well, I'm pretty sure it's not "mail dude." Expecting something?
I haven't gotten a postcard from Bethany in a week.

She's probably just been busy.
She's never gone this long without writing! And the last postcard I sent was really important.

No sulking! I've got a few days off! What'll it be? Concert in the park? Bike ride? Movie?! There's a new nature doc about lemurs, isn't there?

The Wax Museum of Justice.

You *hate* superheroes.
But it'll be . . . educational.

And you know I *haaaate* wax museums.
I saw a TV show that said it's good for you to confront your fears.

Sigh. Fine.

THE WAX MUSEUM OF
JUSTICE
If I'm murdered by an evil wax monster, please avenge my death.

THE WAX MUSEUM OF JUSTICE! Home to 100 percent accurate re-creations of New York City's greatest sidekicks and superheroes!

When do we get to see the Eastern Screech?!

It's official. I've never had a nightmare this bad.

And *this* is one of the biggest milestones. Get your cameras ready, folks!

Ready for . . .

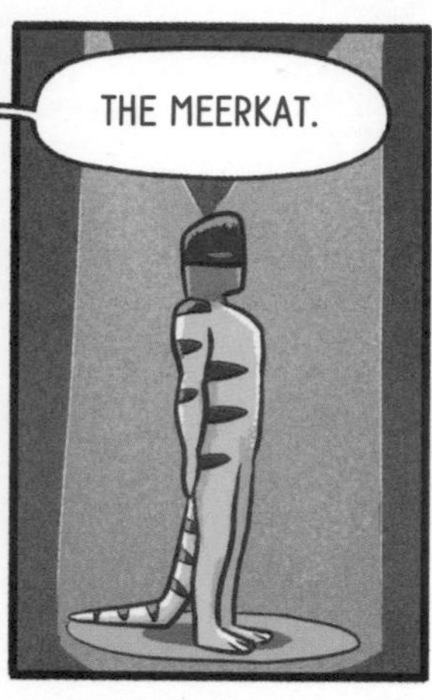
THE MEERKAT.

CLICK

You know The Meerkat! The first super-sidekick? Had the coolest superpowers. Like being able to sit upright for hours, excellent 20/20 vision, and . . .

Is that the Eastern Screech's statue?!

I think it just moved. Did it just move?
When do we get to see the supervillains?

Did you not read the tour descriptions? We don't glorify villains. If you want to see the supervillain room, you have to pay extra for the Goth Tour.

It's too bright in here. It hurts my soul.
I don't even *have* a soul.
One time I saw puppies playing and I, like, didn't smile at all!

Guess we'll skip ahead. Welcome to the Hall of Modern Heroes.

Ah, what do you know. The line for Owl Guy, uh, I mean the Eastern Screech, is super long. Why don't I tell you about a BETTER hero in the meantime!

No way The Anvilator, trademarked, is a better hero than the Eastern Screech.

No, not The Anvilator, trademarked. I'm talking about his sidekick, COLD HANDS!

Want to know a secret?
This is an exact—and I do mean exact—replica of Cold Hands. Yes, that's right. Cold Hands walked these halls, saw the same things you're seeing, and breathed through weird straws up his nose as they made that super itchy wax mold. . . .

I gotta go to the bathroom.
Oh, thank goodness! I'll go with you.

NO!

I mean, I heard there are wax statues in the bathroom.
IN THE BATHROOM?! WHYYYY?!

I'll be back in two minutes.
Okay. Two minutes. I can do this. I'll wait right here.

Or here. Here is better.

I don't even have lights in my apartment.
I go through four eyeliners a day.
I once accidentally bought something dark navy blue, but when I got home and realized it wasn't black, I was like "Oh, nuh-uhhhh." LOL!
SUPERVILLAIN STATUES.
ENTER AT YOUR OWN RISK.

I'm pretty sure it fell off in here.
Are you SURE you're missing one?

. . . fourteen, fifteen.
See? It's gone.

Got it. Phew. It woulda been so embarrassing walking around with only fifteen earrings.

PHEW!

KICK
MOU

AAAAHHH!

HAHAHAHAHAHAHAH

HAHA! Yeah. There's no way that's Ms. Lang. I can't believe I thought she was the Mousetress.

And I can't even tell you the weird places you—I mean, the heroes—find plaster after it's done.

Does anyone have any questions . . .

. . . that AREN'T about the Eastern Screech?

CLICK

I'm telling you, I saw that statue blink! I'm not saying it was alive, but it definitely blinked!
I'm glad I didn't inherit your overactive imagination.

They had an underwear inflator. I wouldn't be surprised if they had some mechanical blinking mechanisms, too.

I love mother-daughter day, and I'm happy to see you smiling, but let's never go there again. Deal?
Deal. I already learned everything I need to.

CHAPTER TEN

Hey, Katie,

OHMIGOD you would not believe what Jessica did! I already told you about Ben, right? Well, I made it super clear that I had a crush on him, but then I went to get more Smores supplies and when I got back Jessica was talking to him! Like after she knew I liked him! She's really getting on my nerves. Please, please, please get here soon!

–Beth

Katie Spera

5965 Ave D, Apt 3B

BETH?!

FWUMP

Hey, Pouty McPoutface.
I got you something.

You've been doing such a good job saving for camp. I wanted to help.

Mom! How . . . ?
Just a few bucks here and there. Let's put down that deposit!

Isn't that Bethany?

No . . . it's BETH.
It's $3,500 a week now?! Why did it go up? How can sleeping in the woods be this expensive?!

I guess the other rate was an early-bird special.
Don't worry. We can still save up the money. . . .

Honey, are you okay?
Yeah, I'm fine. I mean . . .

Do you think I'll have fun at camp?
I mean . . . do you think I'll fit in?
Of course! My Katie Cat can make fun anywhere!
Is this about the postcard?

I didn't read it . . . but I did notice the lack of stickers.

I have to run to work, but remember Bethany loves you and I love you. You'll have so much fun once you get there. You worked hard for this. I'm proud.

LABYRINTH

5B
KNOCK
KNOCK

You're early!

Thank goodness! Save me from eating this entire chocolate cake before it eats me!

Hmm, not my best material, but I think it warranted a bit more than that. You okay?
I'm just having a bad day. Thought the cats could distract me.

Do you want to talk about it?
No.

Look at that. My boss just texted and told me the office has to close. Guess I have the night off.

Okay. I'll go.

Stay. I'm thinking I might whip up some mac and cheese, maybe rent a movie?
That could be nice.

Did you ever have a best friend who suddenly didn't feel like your best friend anymore?
I did. Once. And it was really hard.

I got a postcard from my friend Bethany. First one in weeks. She used to write every day. Now she's just ignoring me. I had written her a really important postcard she didn't even acknowledge! And she signed the card Beth, not Bethany. BETH!
And there's some guy named Ben! UGH, I don't even know if I WANT to go to camp anymore!

I feel like she's changing.

You're changing, too. In good ways. I've been so impressed with you these last few weeks.

But it's like that old saying: "Absence makes the heart grow fungus." Distance is hard. People grow apart. They also grow back together. If she's a good friend, she knows how special you are and that she's lucky to have you.

Thanks, Ms. Lang.
Please. Call me Madeline. All my friends do.

LATER THAT EVENING

siiigh...

Oof.
Stupid online grappling hook course.

Uh, I mean, I meant to miss. Clearly that building is historic and might have been damaged by my powerful throw.

And now I must be off! Cold Hands, away!

OOF!
TRIP

No, wait! Don't go! You work at the Wax Museum, don't you?
Wax? Museum? I've never heard of these words!

But didn't you sit for your sidekick wax cast?
Oh! So you're a *fan.* Let me find something to autograph.

Do you know the Mousetress?

That evil rodent! Of course I do! I've battled her many times. And won! But uh . . . then let her go, because you girls are weak and . . . um . . . gross.

Does she actually look like the wax sculpture in the museum?
Hey! That wasn't part of your tour!

Uh . . . I mean. I assume it wasn't . . .
You said all the statues were 100 percent accurate, but I thought she was shorter. And had less pointy teeth. And had a bunch of cat minions?

Listen, kid. You know no one has ever captured the Mousetress. You really think she'd voluntarily sit in a chair for hours with straws up her nose getting a wax figure made so unappreciative tourists can take selfies with it?

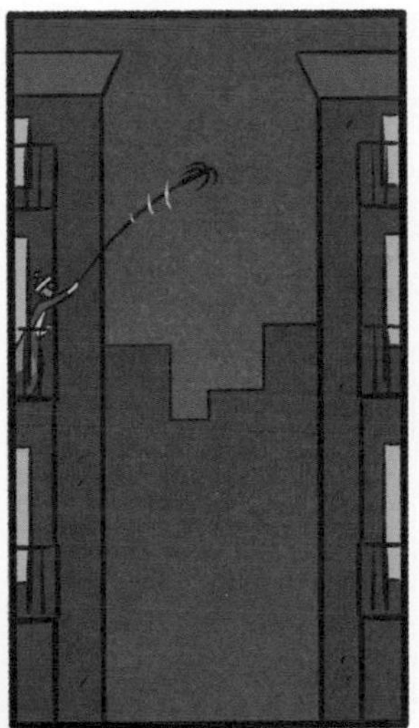
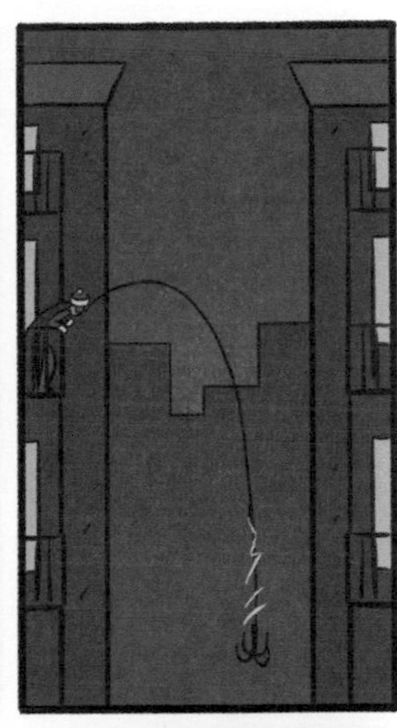

Uh. Keep it.
College fund.

Mousetress sightings

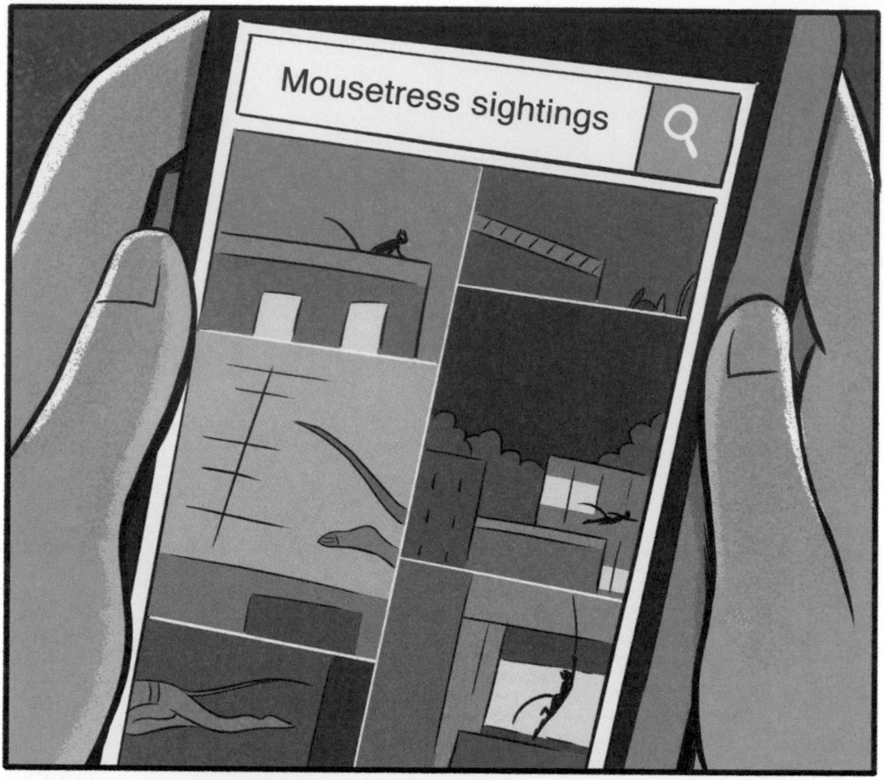

Mousetress sightings

You're still awake?

Do you think it's possible for someone to be evil and good at the same time?
Is this still about the postcard?

MOM!
I promised I didn't *read* it. It just seemed off. Is everything okay?

It's not about Bethany.

I think Ms. Lang might be the Mousetress.

I think we'd know if the worst supervillain in New York City lived two floors above us!
But that's the thing. I don't think she's a villain at all.

Well, in that case, I hope she'll put some of that stolen money from all those diamond thefts toward fixing our building's leaky roof.
Phew!

Remember the chocolate? It was from PURE ORGANIC the day the factory had that explosion.
You don't think that's a coincidence?

Your imagination is something.

Come on. Get some sleep. Tomorrow is a big day.

It's . . .

CHAPTER ELEVEN

PICKLE
WORLDS SPICIEST PICKLE!
Ready?
Never.

CRUNCH

It's . . .
good?

Horses are noble!
HA HA

Our country was founded on horses, and you can bet George Washington gave his horses food and a bath!

Hey, it's Ms. Lang.
Ha. You mean THE MOUSETRESS!

Let's go say hi.

Katie! Cheryl! So good to see you here!
We were actually just at Pickle Fest.
Also a very noble cause!
What are you protesting?

Mistreatment of the carriage horses in the city. Those horses sleep in boxes so small they can't even lie down. Sometimes I feel like holding up a sign isn't enough.
But it's comforting to realize you aren't alone.

I basically landed it!
BUMP
You totally didn't land it.

Sorry about that! I'm normally really good at ollies.
No, you aren't.

She doesn't know that, Nicole!

Cool to see another kid at the protest! I feel like we're always the only ones.
I was just passing by and ran into my friend Ms. Lang.

You know Ms. Lang?! She's the coolest. Do you want to know a secret about her? I think she's secretly . . .

Stainless Steel!

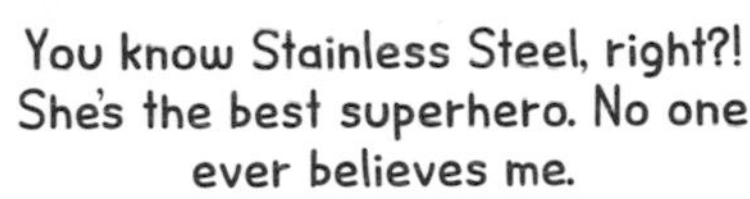
You know Stainless Steel, right?! She's the best superhero. No one ever believes me.
But Ms. Lang is smart, super athletic, and always fighting for what's right. She has to be Stainless Steel!

Maybe?
More than maybe! And one day I'll prove it!

Ooh, look! It's her turn.

Last week it was 98 degrees with a heat index of 104. I didn't leave my air-conditioned home. I'm sure you didn't. But Jack was forced to leave his "home"—a box truck so small he can't even turn around. Jack is a carriage horse.
He was only out for an hour when he collapsed. His handler said he tripped, but you all saw the video. We're here because it's time to start treating animals the way they treat us.
In 1918, a female soldier became one of the most decorated World War I heroes. She saved 197 lives by flying a message over enemy lines. Yes, you heard me right. FLYING. That war hero . . . was a pigeon.
Animals have saved people from gas leaks, fires, heart attacks, diabetic comas, hypothermia, falling into deep wells.

I know you are probably imagining Lassie right now, and yes, some of these stories are about dogs, but there are also stories of cats, pigs, rabbits, gorillas, wolves, and even dolphins saving people.
Animals are intelligent. They have emotions. They can be loyal. They can be brave.
People always talk about treating animals in a humane way . . . but I think we need to do better than that, because we definitely don't treat other humans in a humane way.
Like Jack, we walk around with blinders on, but unlike Jack, we have a choice. Thank you all for joining in this rally to spread kindness to every living thing in this great city of ours.

Gotta go. See ya around! We're the Wheel-las. Look us up! We're here every day.
KLAK

I'm Marie, by the waaaaaay.
OOF

I was hoping you'd meet Marie. She's a great kid.
She seems cool.
Meant to do that!

It's getting late. I've got a big night at the office. See you at six o'clock, Katie?
I'll be there!

CHAPTER TWELVE

I'll take 217 . . .
MEOW
. . . 218 of your finest cat treats.

On the house.

I'll never understand how you can pay rent when you constantly give things away for free.
Actually, I don't pay rent.

How?!
Don't tell anyone . . . but Benito Benton is my brother.

The billionaire?!
When our grandparents passed, they left half the money to him and half to me.

YOU'RE A BILLIONAIRE?!

Naw. Not anymore. Bought this building, and there were a lot of places that needed donations.
Why would you even work?

Sometimes you do things because it makes you happy. Not because it makes you money.

And on that note, here's a special Mr. B PB&J at the friends and family 100 percent off discount. Don't tell your mom.
I like to keep an air of mystery around me.

Hey, still think Madeline is a supervillain?

No.
Definitely not.

This time . . . I'm gonna win.

Who's in for board game night?

5 HOURS AND 59 MINUTES LATER
You're just lucky Madeline will be home in a minute or I'd TOTALLY win the rematch.

11:59

12:00

Madeline! You gotta teach Scrabbles that it's not cool to cheat.

Okay. That's . . . weird.

Everyone is late now and then. There's nothing to worry . . .
CLICK

I'm here with the Eastern Screech, whose Yelp rating has just skyrocketed with the latest news.

Eastern Screech, tell us what happened.

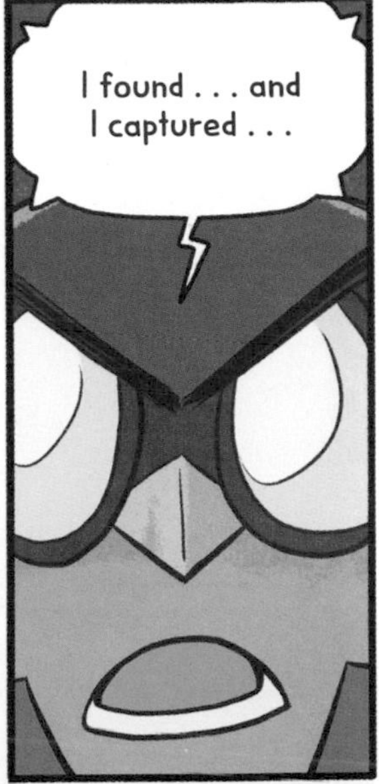

THE MOUSETRESS.

Sadly, despite her capture, the Mousetress has yet to be unmasked. Seems her goggles are held on with some sort of high-tech mechanism.
I'm working on that. I can science, too.

Madeline is just running late. That's not her.

Like Mr. B says, I've got an overactive . . .

FLICK

THUNK

. . . imagination.

MEOW
MEOW
MIAV

CLICK!

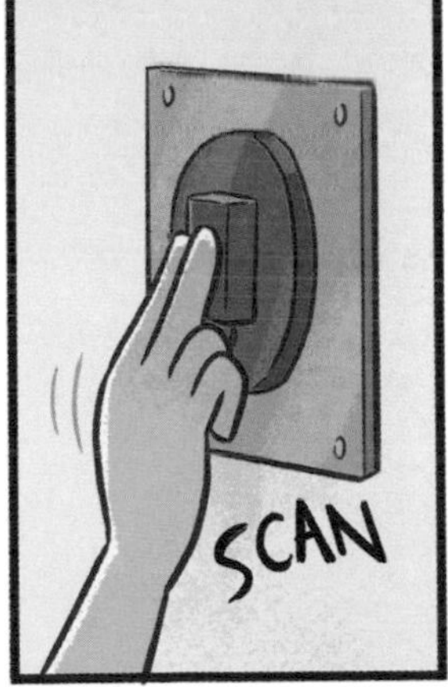
SCAN

~PSSSTTT

Whoa.

What are you doing?

I'm not a superhero! Or villain or whatever! I'm just a kid! There's nothing I can do.

PRISON FLOOR PLAN
TAP
TAP
TAPPITY
TAPPITY
TAP
TAP

Meow meow meow meow!

PRISON FL

MEOW MEOW!
MEOW MEOW!
MEEEOW!!

Yeah. I still don't
speak cat.

Wow, Frida, you are a GREAT artist. Is this the prison . . . and all of you . . . and me?
And a window near Madeline's cell?
Only six guards?
I can actually understand this!

You're right.
Let's save Madeline.

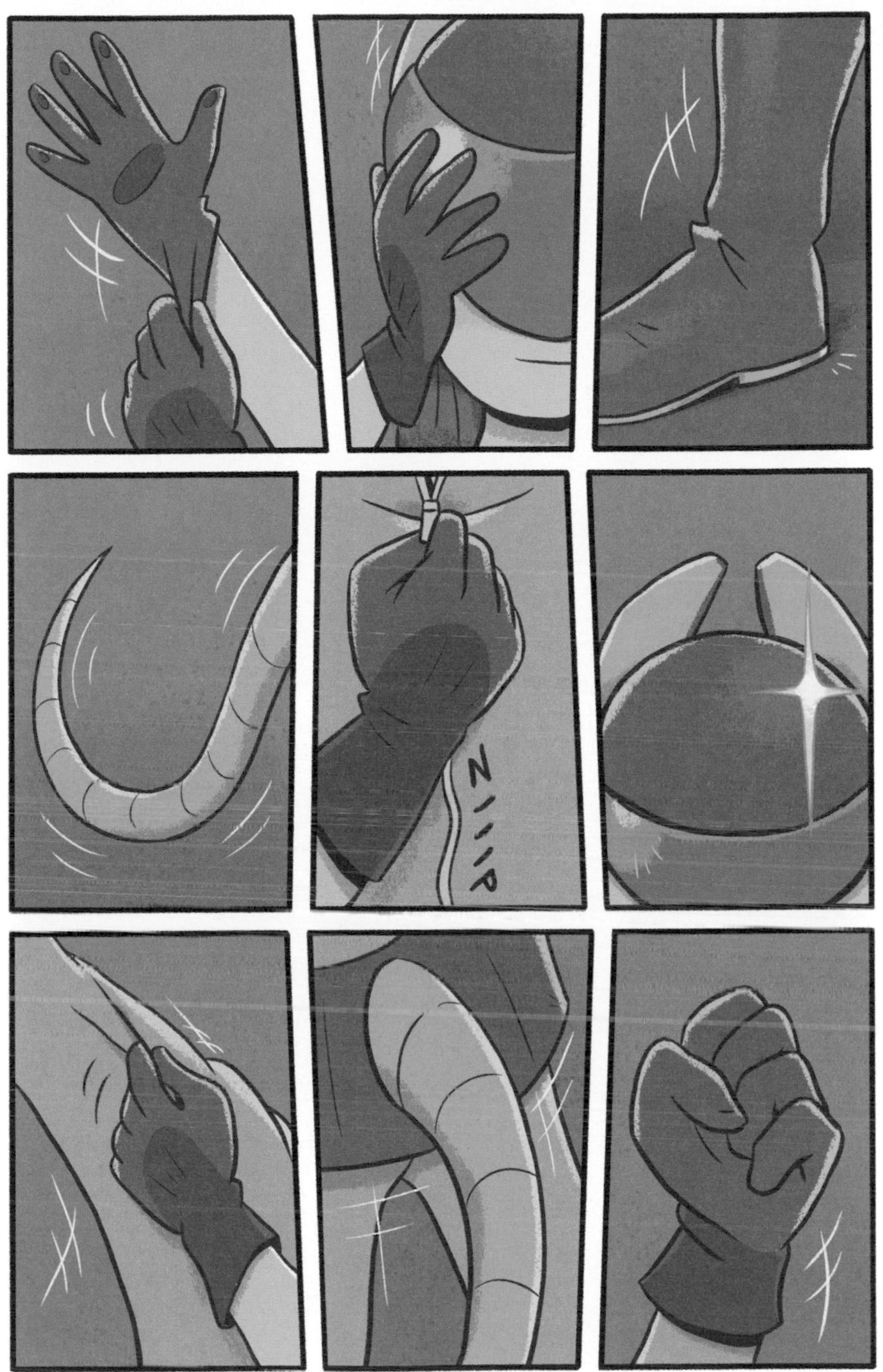
ZIIIP

Here we go!

ACK!
TRIP

SEW
SEW
SEW

PTHOO!

SMASH

Oops.
Uh . . . Kitty roll call!

Jolie: Computer Hacking

Gracie: Language Expert
Myau.

Moritz: Counterattacks

Miles: Laser Expert

Hildy:
Super-Speed Reflexes

Chaz: YouTube Tutorials

General Titus:
Super Strength

Frida: Master Artist

Peeve: Military Strategist

Captain Von Smooch:
Audiovisual Expert

Curly:
Expert Seamstress

Jack Slayer:
Getaway Driver

Paw Simon:
Splitting Up Teams

Pierogi: Textiles Expert

Nox: Robotics Expert

Puff: Smoke Bombs

Dr. Claw: Bath Bombs

Lyapa: Weapons Expert

Smushy:
Mixed Martial Arts

Bentley: Sonic Purr

Seamus: Math Genius

Lasagna:
Camouflage Expert

DJ Bootie Butler:
Mad Beats

Ahhh! We don't have time for this! We need to go save Madeline!

CHAPTER THIRTEEN

Aaaaahhh! It's the Mousetress!!!!

How do you get this . . .

SWIPE!

Scratch-Off! You're one of Madeline's, too?!

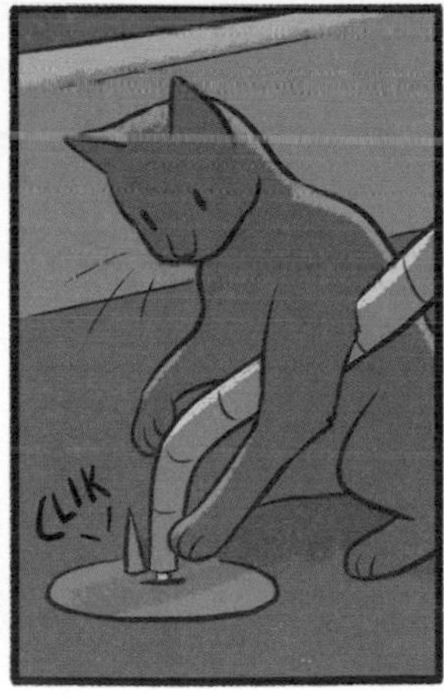
CLIK

WHOA.

BZZZ!!
WHIIR

Hi, Mom.
I just got the strangest call from Mrs. Piper.
WIIIRRR

Stranger than usual? Is that even possible? Heh. Heh.
WHIIIRRR

She's convinced she saw the Mousetress climbing the building—going on and on about giant claws, glowing red eyes . . .
Didn't Owl Guy just catch her?
WIIIIRRR

All I know is she seemed really scared . . . almost concerned, which is definitely not like her.
WHIIIIIRRR

Just promise me you'll stay with the cats. They'll keep you safe.
WIIIRRR

I promise.

I can do this. I can totally do this. I've played video games like this.

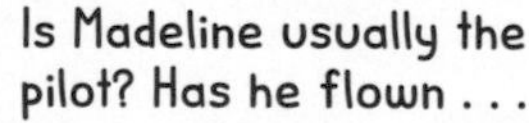

Is Madeline usually the pilot? Has he flown . . .

. . . BEFOOORE?

Wow.

Let's review the plan! Frida's drawing says there are six guards stationed by Madeline's cell. Dr. Claw, Paw Simon, and Prince of Space, you distract them.
When the coast is clear, Miles will navigate the laser system. Once he gets to the control panel, Jolie will shut down the alarm. I'll climb in and use my mouse tail to undo the lock!

You know, this mission doesn't actually sound impossible! Ha!

What?

What happened to
SIX guards?!

TAP TAP TAPPITITY
TAP
TAPPITY
TAP
TAP
TAP
TAP

I can't believe he's here!
I know! It's my day off, but I came in! Does my hair look okay?

CLICK

I became a prison guard just so I could meet him one day!
Ha! So I guess you're quitting tomorrow.
Whoa.

Yes.
What?
I don't know. It's like Owl Guy didn't trust us to watch the Mousetress. I find it kind of insulting.

Did you just call him OWL GUY?!
Hold me back! Hold me back!

Seriously.
Someone hold me.
Seamus,
how many are
there?

6 GUARDS
44 + 1
OWL DUDE

Where's
Owl Guy?

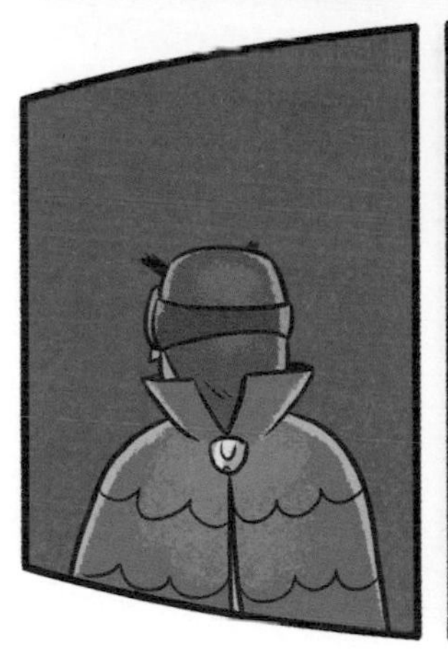

AH!

I will never get used to that.
I've got an idea.
Jolie, can you piece together parts of Owl Guy's TV interviews?
Meow.
Curly, do you have your sewing supplies?
Meow.
Nox, how many mice can you make in the next ten minutes?
Meow.
DJ Bootie Butler, can you tap into the prison's audio system?
Meow.
I'm just gonna hope that meow means a high number.
Frida, can you paint Owl Guy's mask?
Meow.

Okay, on three . . .
"For Madeline!"

One . . .
two . . .
three . . .

FOR MADELINE!
MEOW MEOW
POUR MEOW!!!

I AM THE EASTERN SCREECH
AND I . . .
HERE . . .
NOW!

All right, Jolie, DJ.
Do your thing.
Nox, Frida, Curly,
you ready?

I can't wait to meet the Eastern Screech and finally quit working here! Maybe I'll be a baker? A dog walker? A YouTube star with my own unboxing channel? I mean, dream the dream, am I right?
Where *is* he? I was told he'd sign my book!

Maybe he's *actually* guarding the prisoner, like we should be?

Sniff sniff. Um, is that a lavender bath bomb?
Dibs!
Wrong one! Wrong one!

What in the . . .

THE EASTERN SCREECH!

He's here!
What an entrance!

YES, IT IS I. EASTERN SCREECH. HELLO, CITIZENS. LOOKING GOOD. I LIKE UNIFORMS.

WHAT WEATHER! WHO WANT AUTOGRAPH?
SEW
SEW
SEW
SEW

Me! Me! I have your book!
I have your *New York Times* article!
I have your limited-edition action figure with 270-degree head rotation and action punch arm!
I have a strand of your hair!!!
CLIK

Whal?
PHTOOOO

It's working!
PLEASE KEEP LINE. PLENTY SCREECH FOR ALL. I LOVE CATS!

Huuuuurrk.
HAIRBALL!

Superheroes are so cool!
I wish I could make my head fall off!

Sign my book!
Sign my strand of hair!
Sign my action figure!

Huh?
Are our pants sewn together?
Man, I put my pants on really wrong!

Your time to shine, Pierogi!

KNIT KNIT KNIT KNIT KNIT KNIT KNIT
KNIT KNIT
KNIT KNIT KNIT KNIT
KNIT KNIT

Pom-poms are a nice touch!

CHAPTER FOURTEEN

Hickory dickory dock, look at your clock . . . because if you could tell time, you are out of it. Time, that is.

Let's make magic,
Miles.

Well, that works, too.

HUFF
CLICK

We got it! Madeli—
Uh . . . I mean, THE MOUSETRESS?

Katie?! Is that you?!

It's me! Are you okay?! We're going to get you out!

I do not think that is what is going to happen.

CRUSH

NINJA SQUAD, GO!

WEAPONS SQUAD, GO!

MMA SQUAD, GO!

WRESTLING SQUAD, GO!

Uh . . . Gymnast Squad, go?

Cat minions following a giant evil mouse? So pathetic.

The Mousetress isn't evil! She was just trying to help animals!

Oh, I know that. But have you seen my Yelp rating lately? This capture is great press. It's time to give up, little mouse girl.
I'm the greatest hero this city has ever known. There's no way a bunch of cats, an oversized mouse, and . . .

. . . a little girl—scoff—could ever defeat—
MORITZ! COUNTERATTACK!

BONK

Meeeeee?
YAWN

That lock needs two keys turned at the same time, plus two authorized fingerprints at opposite sides of the room. There's no way you're going to open it.

Help the animals. Yeah, figured that out a while back. I'm a huge fan of her work, and I know Fluffernutter and Sophie are, too.

Wait, what if there were TWO of you?!
Huh?
Give me your hand!

SCAN

VRRT VRRT

Ready?
One . . .
Two . . .

Three!

SHWOOP

PURR
PURR
PURR
PURR
PURR
PURR

Thank you for your service, Mousetress.

You saved me, Mousetress. I wuv youuuu!

Uh. Anyways. Use the back staircase, and maybe don't mention this to my boss?

What about the camera footage? Won't you get in trouble?
Somehow the cameras stopped working a few minutes before I got here. Weird coincidence.

Go home, you two!

And another thing . . .

BONK

Big owl man is taking a big ol' nap. Wook at that sweepy owl man!

CHAPTER FIFTEEN

I'm going to take a break from my night shift for a while. Focus on ways I can fight injustice during the day.

Here, you earned this. It's the rest of the money for camp, and a few extra things I thought you might like.

My own Mousetress goggles?!

And this. Have you ever been to a Straight from the Farm?
You mean that super-fancy vegan place I definitely can't afford? Haha. Nope.

That card gets free food for life. Just promise me you'll occasionally get something other than PB&J.

How did . . . ?
I own them. All of them. And you now own part of them, too. Or at least you will when you turn eighteen.

New York City is lucky to have a hero like you, Katie. Have an amazing time at camp.

A FEW DAYS LATER
Are you SURE you packed everything?

Yes, I'm sure. Don't worry, Mom. I'll be fine!
I know, it's just this is all new for me!

Promise me you'll text.
Every hour.

You ready?
Oh! I almost forgot, a postcard from Bethany arrived earlier.

I'll read it later. Love you, Mom!

I'm gonna get you, Mousetress! Climb up MY building. I don't think so.

SNATCH!

Haunted! This building is haunted!

FUND
Katie! We had a superhero day, and the Eastern Screech showed up. He's really not that bad! Kinda cute, almost. AND he was with Stainless Steel! She was so cool, and I feel like I really knew her right away! I can't believe you aren't coming to camp this year. But next year for sure, right? Hope you aren't too bored!
Love ya —Beth
Katie Spera
5963 Ave D Apt 3B
New York, NY 10009

VET SCHOOL
~~CAMP~~
FUND

FUND

Katie! We had a superhero day, and the Eastern Screech showed up. He's really not that bad! Kinda cute, almost. AND he was with Stainless Steel! She was so cool, and I feel like I really knew her right away! I can't believe you aren't coming to camp this year. But next year for sure, right? Hope you aren't too bored!

Love ya —Beth

Katie Spera
5965 Ave D, Apt 3B
New York, NY 10009

And then you just push your leg like this . . . no, wait, like THIS.

Haha!

The ~~End~~ Beginning

Don't miss the next

Katie the Catsitter, Best Friends for Never—

coming in 2022!

MEET COLLEEN!

© Amber Harrison

COLLEEN AF (ANN FELICITY) VENABLE

grew up in Walden, New York. She's a lifelong comic book fan, maker, and roller-skater, and was the designer for multiple award-winning graphic novels at First Second Books. She is also the author of the Guinea Pig Pet Shop Private Eye series and numerous acclaimed picture books, and was longlisted for a National Book Award for her YA graphic novel debut, *Kiss Number 8*. Colleen's making her middle-grade debut with *Katie the Catsitter*. She lives in Brooklyn, New York, with her pet bunnies, Tuck and Cher, and occasionally starts national holidays. (True story!) Visit Colleen online at colleenaf.com and @colleenaf.

I would never have 217 cats. That's just silly. I'd keep it to under 50. Maybe 75. Plus 42 dogs, 77 rabbits, 91 fish, 86 guinea pigs, 33 sugar gliders, and a single capybara. (They're big. It would be ridiculous to have more than one!) I live in a tiny apartment in New York City with a fish that is 17 years old and two amazing bunnies—one is convinced he's a dog, and the other is convinced she's a cat. They come when I call their names and can open puzzle boxes to get treats. They're well on their way to genius minion status.

The only thing I love more than comic books is helping animals. I'm an adoption counselor for a local animal rescue, and it's my dream to help animals all around the world by volunteering with scientists and animal hospitals.

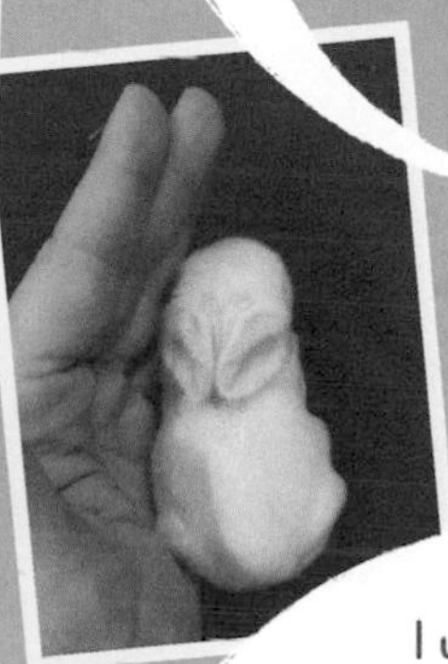

I wrote this book because I love animals, and because I wanted there to be more cool female superheroes, but I also wanted to tell a story about how hard it is when you and your best friend start to grow apart. Bethany (BETH?!) and Katie's friendship was inspired by my own childhood friendship breakups. Just remember, for every friend you drift away from, there are so many more out there who would be honored to have you in their life.

COLLEEN AT 12!

And who knows? Maybe those friends will even help you accidentally co-create a national holiday like mine did. Happy Pancake Day/Lumberjack Day (every September 26)!

© Timothy Wade Jr.

MEET STEPH!

STEPHANIE YUE grew up in Atlanta, Beijing, and Hong Kong. She's a lifetime comics fan and martial artist (with a black belt in kung fu) and travels the world by motorbike. Stephanie is the illustrator of the Guinea Pig Pet Shop Private Eye series and several picture books and chapter books, and was the colorist of *Smile* by Raina Telgemeier. She is making her debut as a middle-grade graphic novel illustrator with *Katie the Catsitter.* Stephanie currently divides her time between Hong Kong, San Francisco, Lisbon, and Boston, where she's working on the second *Katie the Catsitter* graphic novel. Visit her online at stephanieyue.com and on Twitter at @quezzie.

I definitely wanted to be a superhero when I grew up. It's probably why I got into kung fu, and then Muay Thai, and now Brazilian jiujitsu. I still have time, right?

DEOSAI PLAINS, PAKISTAN

CHICKEN, ALASKA

I love adventure and travel. When I learned to ride a motorcycle it opened up a whole new way to explore the world. I love riding and I want to ride the world! Can you tell the Mousetress's costume was inspired by motorcycle gear?

Katie the Catsitter was illustrated from Hong Kong, Chiang Mai, Boston, Barcelona, and Lisbon, among other places. My portable studio is small enough to fit into a backpack and set up almost anywhere. I even take it on the bike with me!

Chaz:
Cleopatra:
Admiral Dewey: Tea Expert
Apollo: Space Travel Expert
Baby Teefling: Supernatural Historian
Bear Aspirin: Veterinarian
Bentley: Sonic Purr
Boumi: Haberdasher
Cat Benatar: Lead Vocals
Chester C. Wombat: Politics
Clog: Design Expert
Albie: Graphic Novel Expert
Archibald: Historian
Bailey: Expert Hunter
Beebs LaRue: Hip Hop Dance
Bimpers: Tap Dancing
Bugsy: Pickpocketing
Cathulhu: Luchador
Chomsky: Cognitive Science
Cobweb: Interior Decorator
Angstrom: Chemist
Athena: Super Speed
Bandit: Sleight-of-Paw Magic
Beedee: High Jump
Blanche: Fundraisers
Calia: Bouldering
Catman Crothers: Actor
Clara Joy: Geography Expert
Cringer: Skateboard Master
Auggie: Jump Rope Master
Bartholomew: Climate Change Activist
Belladonna: Roller-skating
Bobo Baggins: Rokushaku Bō
Captain Von Smooch: Audiovisual Expert
Chairman Meow: Arm Wrestling Champ
Claudia: Cellular Technology
Curly: Expert Seamstress

Diavolessa: Opera Singer
DJ Bootie Butler: Mad Beats
Pastry Chef
Ella: Contortionist
Eggs & Bacon: Master Chef
Dustbunny: Allergist
Dr. Motorcycle: Judo
Dr. Claw: Bath Bombs
Domino: Coding Expert
Françoise: Vlogger
Fiddlesticks: Woodworker
Feral Francis: Needlepoint
Esme: Bodybuilding
Em-Dash: Grammar Expert
Elvis: Faking Your Death
Giuseppe: Tightrope Wal
Gidget: Surfing Expert
Georgie: Optics Expert
General Titus: Super Strength
Frida: Master Artist
Frankie Thunder-kitten: Cartoonist
Gollumpus: Iron Man Competitions
Gordon P. Kitty: Geology Expert
Gracie: Language Expert
Grampy: Ballet Dance
Grimlock: Photographer
Hashbrown: Composting Expert
Hazel: Paper Engineering
Higgins: Book Agent
Hildy: Super-Speed Reflexes
Izzy: Comedy Historian
Jack Slayer: Getaway Driver
Jervous: Window Washing
Jolie: Computer Hacking
CLASSIFIED
Knee-Knee: Screen Printing
Knope: Organizing Community Action
Lakshmi: Accounting
Leer: Staring Contests
Little Lil: Author
Lizbeth: Puppeteer
DO NOT OPEN

Expert
Lwax: Candlemaking
Lyapa: Weapons Expert
Lucy: Jet Pilot
Mackerel: Semaphore Expert
Mariposa: Photographic Memory
Marla: Karaoke
Maxi: Art Curator
Footwe
Marley: Murder Podcast Expert
arlowe: Architect
urka: Teacher
Meat Throwin
Marmalade: Beekeeper
Max: Charisma
Melrose: Aircraft Engineer
Meowth von Lan Fourth : Fitnes
topheles: nomer
Merlin: Fashion Designer
Mew Mew: Costumes
Miles: Laser Expert
Minnie: Publicity
Miss Moon: Video Game Expert
Moe: Crafts and Glue Guns
Moogle: Construction
Moritz: Counterattacks
Mr. Aaron Purr Sir: Duels
Mr. Pickles: Jiujitsu
Mr. Smackers: Legume Farmer
Mrs. Kensington: Botanist
Neko: Fire Safety Technician

nan:
echanic

Nick Furry:
Comic Book Historian

Niko: Ankle Attacks

Niles: Podcaster

Noodle: Advertising

botics Expert

Nugget: Astrophysicist

Obediah: Marine Biologist

Olav:
Ceramics Master

Olive Loaf: Animato

lo: Movie Expert

P Jammies: Prototyping

Partly Cloudy:
Meteorologist

Pavement:
Physics Expert

Paw Simon:
Splitting Up Tea

Peake:
Location Specialist

Pearl Mae:
Biomedical Engineer

Peeve:
Military Strategist

Penny:
Movie Director

Pepper:
Electrical Re

Pesco: Financial Analyst

Phil: Rock Climber

Pierogi: Textiles Expert

Pigeon: Baseball Expert

Pika:
Muay T

Pippen:
Ergonomics Expert

Pixel: Organizing Groups

Poe: Lock Picking

Polly Jean:
Cryptologist

Pop
Endod

Potato:
Yoga Instructor

Precious: Super Gas

Prince Namor: Librarian

Prince of Space:
Helicopter Repair

Princ
Fore

Prune Juice:

Puff: Smoke Bombs

Puss N Cahoots: Lawyer

Gla

Raven:
Alternative Fuels Expert
Reba: Jeweler
Rigby:
Industrial Engineer
Rory:
History of Televi
Rose: Super Smell
Ruth:
Classical Music Expert
Rylan: Free Solo Climbing
Sadie:
Brazilian Jiujitsu
Sassafras Assassin:
Graphic Designer
Scrabbles: Board Games
Scratch-Off:
Small Business Expert
Seamus: Math Genius
Shamrock:
Green Initiatives
Shrimpy Longstockings:
Makeup Artist
Shuffleboard: Sea Captain
Sir!: Expert Skier
Siren:
Forensics
Smushy: Mixed Martial Arts
Snag: Mechanical Engineering
Sniff:
Radiologis
wball:
gy Specialist
Speed-B:
Asphalt Maintenance
Spooky Punkin Patch:
Ghost Stories
Squea
Talent Sc
rling:
rologist
Stevie: Oceanographer
Stuart:
Motorcycle Maintenance
Sunshine:
Toxicologist

Sushi:
Wind Energy Expert
Tammy Faye:
Floor Gymnastics
Tesla:
Giving Ideas Away
The Cuteness:
Welding
Thwomp: Musician
Tiki Birdmin:
Pizza-ologist
Tortie:
Nanotechnology
Trax:
Renewable Energy Expert
Triana: Ninja
Trillan: Decoys
Velcro:
Statistics
TOP SECRET
Vinnie Van G:
Tag Team Wrestler
Viola:
Soap Opera Expert
Wicket:
Mass Transit Expert
Willow Harkill:
Photonics Engineer
Wisteria:
Existential Theories
Wolfgang Catclops:
Housekeeping
Xerxes: Hidden Cameras
Zizzy: Indie Filmmaker
Zo-Zo:
Furniture Designer
Zucca: Acrobat

Gracie, the language expert, can meow in eighty-two languages. Here are some of the ways to speak cat around the world!

muwaa
(Arabic)

miav
(Danish)

miaou
(French)

miau
(German)

myau
(Hebrew)

miyaun
(Hindi)

meow
(English)

nyan
(Japanese)

yaong
(Korean)

miao
(Mandarin)

myau
(Russian)

miau
(Spanish)

miyav
(Turkish)